It's a beautiful day in the city, and Spider-Man is cruising down the street, making sure all is well in the neighborhood. Suddenly, he receives a call for help. "Spider-Man, we need you!"

Meanwhile, just a few blocks away, Green Goblin is busy hurling pumpkins from his window, narrowly missing his neighbors and passing cars!

"Ha, ha!" Green Goblin laughs with delight as each pumpkin smashes into pieces. "No one can smash pumpkins better than me!"

Spidey races to the scene, arriving just in time to catch a flying pumpkin in his web.

"Hold it right there, Green Goblin!" Spidey warns.
"Just try and stop me!" Green Goblin replies. "This is fun!"

"But look at the mess you are making!" Spidey scolds. "Not to mention that what you're doing is dangerous and people could get hurt."

"Who cares!?" cries Green Goblin. And with that, he jumps on his glider and soars through the sky, hurling pumpkin after pumpkin to the ground below.

Surprised by the storm of pumpkins, Spidey manages to catch just one in his web, while the others smash around him, splashing him with pumpkin mush.
"I think it's time Green Goblin learns a valuable lesson," Spidey decides.

The next day, Green Goblin spots a moving van pulling up to the house next door. "New neighbors! What fun!" he exclaims. "I think a smashed-pumpkin welcome is in order!"

Just then, the moving van pulls away, revealing Green Goblin's new neighbor...
Spider-Man! "What are *you* doing here!?" Green Goblin asks, very unhappily.
"Just your friendly neighborhood Spider-Man," Spidey replies. "And I'm moving in!"

Green Goblin storms back inside his house. "If he thinks he's going to ruin all my pumpkin-smashing fun," he grumbles, "he needs to think again!"

Quickly, Green Goblin gets back to work, hurling pumpkin after pumpkin out of his front window, laughing with delight.

But instead of the usual chaos, Green Goblin hears laughter and music coming from the street.

He jumps on his glider and races outside to find a neighborhood Pumpkin Festival going on, filled with pumpkin pies, pumpkin breads, pumpkin muffins – even a pumpkin-eating contest – all with *his* pumpkins!

Green Goblin is outraged! "How can this be? Where are all of my smashed pumpkins? Where is all of the pumpkin mush!?"

Spidey turns to Green Goblin and gives him a thumbs-up.
"Thanks for all the great pumpkins, Green Goblin." This Pumpkin Festival
sure is making good use of them!"

Now Green Goblin is furious! "My pumpkins aren't for festivals! They're for smashing! And I'm the world's best pumpkin smasher!" "Well then, *I'm* the world's best pumpkin catcher!" Spidey says. "And I'll make you a deal. I'll bet you that I can catch every one of your pumpkins. If I win, you have to clean up all the old pumpkin mush in the neighborhood – and stop throwing pumpkins at your neighbors!"

"And if *I* win," Green Goblin responds, "You have to move away and leave me alone! Catch!" Green Goblin hurls one pumpkin after another at Spidey, who catches every one.

"He'll never be able to catch a hundred pumpkins at once!" Green Goblin laughs as he races to the front window and pulls it open…unleashing one hundred pumpkins all at once!

But they're no match for Spider-Man! Spidey quickly throws out both of his webs, making a giant net – that catches every last pumpkin!

"A deal's a deal," Spidey tells Green Goblin as he seals up his window with his super-Spidey web. "It's about time you learned how to be a good neighbor – and how to keep your neighborhood clean!"

"You may have won *this* time, Spider-Man," Green Goblin replies. "I may not be able to smash pumpkins in *this* neighborhood...but there are plenty of others! So watch out, cuz you never know where I'll pop up next!"